Honey and Co

Collection - Books 1 to 4

E. L. Reading

This book belongs to: ....

Honey and Coco
find Santa's presents

Honey and Coco
were playing in the snow,
when Coco saw a celestial glow.

Coco asked, "Who could that be?
There's a jolly laugh coming
from behind that tree."

"Ho, ho, ho," the
man with a white beard said,
standing near a sleigh
painted gold and red.

"Oh no, oh my,
I seem to have lost my way.
I'll never find the presents
that fell from the sleigh."

"Oh," said the man,
"it's Honey and Coco.
I'm in a bit of a
pickle. Ho, ho, ho."

"Yes, we heard," Coco said.
"We were playing in the snow, but we'd rather help you instead."

Santa said,
"You're so good and kind.
I hope we can find
all the presents in time.

Making all of the
gifts takes me a year,
and now I do not know if
they are far or near."

"Do not worry, do not fear,
to me the task ahead seems clear,"

Honey said. "We will help refill your sleigh, and find the presents before the break of day."

Coco said, "We'll be quick. We'll be fast.
Where did you see the presents last?"

Santa said, "That'd
be my very own workshop,
but we must hurry. We cannot stop."

Santa said, "Oh, but of course!
There is Logan's rocking horse."

Coco barked, "Look over there.
That looks like Amelia's teddy bear."

Honey peeked out
from under Santa's red coat.
"I can see Emma's little toy boat."

Coco asked,
"Where next should we look?"
Santa replied, "The perfect place
to find a lost book."

Honey barked,
"Can you give me a lift?
I can see Oliver's special gift."

Coco asked, "Where do you think the next one will be?" Santa replied, "Perhaps it fell when I swerved to avoid a tree?"

Coco approached the large candy cane,
spotting Mia's wooden toy train.

Santa said, "Come on, follow me.
I'm sure I know where the next one will be."

Coco said, "I can see another toy,
underneath a sleeping boy."

Santa said, "Shush. Two left to go.
Follow me quickly, don't be slow."

Santa led them to his bag.
Coco's tail started to wag.

"I am confused," Honey did exclaim,
"this has a bow, but no tag or a name?"

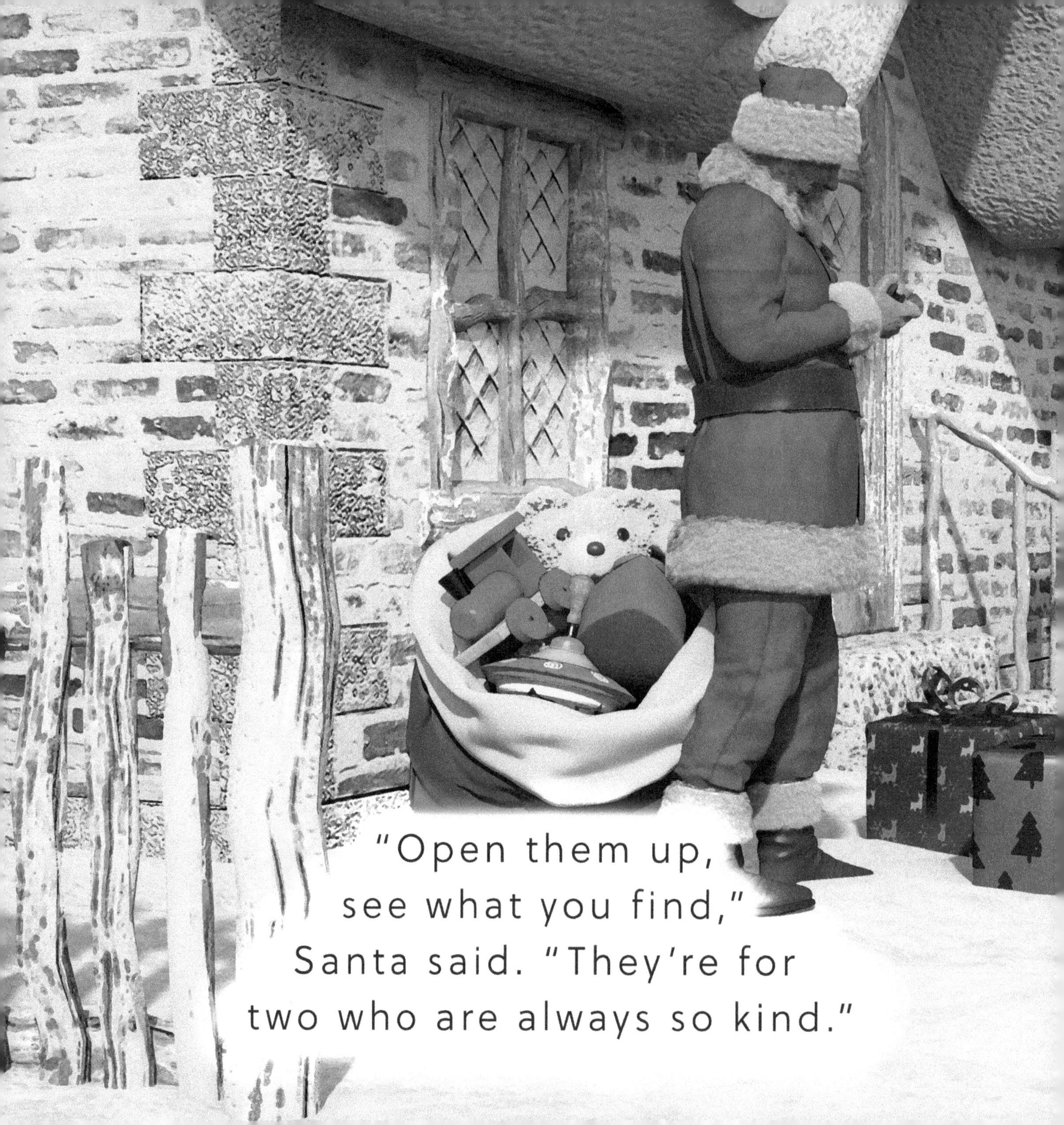

"Open them up,
see what you find,"
Santa said. "They're for
two who are always so kind."

Honey said, "Oh this cannot be?
One is for Coco, and one is for me?"

"I have seen that you are
kind and helpful.
You helped me tonight,
and you're truly delightful."

Santa said, "You've helped others too.
So, yes, these gifts are just for you."

Santa said, "Honey,
you are never selfish,
and for this, I got you your
very own dish.

Coco, my dear,
you always bring joy,
and for this I got you your
own squeaky toy."

Honey said, "Thank you so much. You are very kind. We will always be happy to help anytime."

Honey and Coco's
joyful barks filled the night,
as Santa's sleigh disappeared
from sight.

Spot the difference

Can you find the 5 differences?

Honey and Coco
meet a squirrel

The sun was shining, warm and bright,
much to Honey and Coco's delight.
In the garden, the two did play,
as they did almost every day.

In the trees beyond the fence,
something rustled, making Coco tense.

"Oh, it's you," she said with relief,
toward the orange face behind the leaf.

"Yes, it's me," the squirrel said,
"or perhaps it was this tree instead?"

Coco barked, "Come down and play."
The squirrel laughed, "No chance, no way!"

The squirrel said, "You'll eat me whole,
like a side dish in your bowl."

"No, here's an idea more to my taste.
I'll challenge you to a race."

Honey shook her head and said,
"No. This is silly. Ignore him instead."

"I'm fast," said Coco, "and really quick.
I'll beat that squirrel in just a tick."

With a flash of his
tail, the squirrel was gone.
Coco knew the race was on.

"I'll chase him fast, just you see,"
Coco laughed, filled with glee.

"Oh, what luck the gate is open.
I think the lock must still be broken.
I'll catch that squirrel, you'll soon see.
Then I'll be back in time for tea."

The squirrel leapt between the trees.
Flicking his tail, he landed with ease.

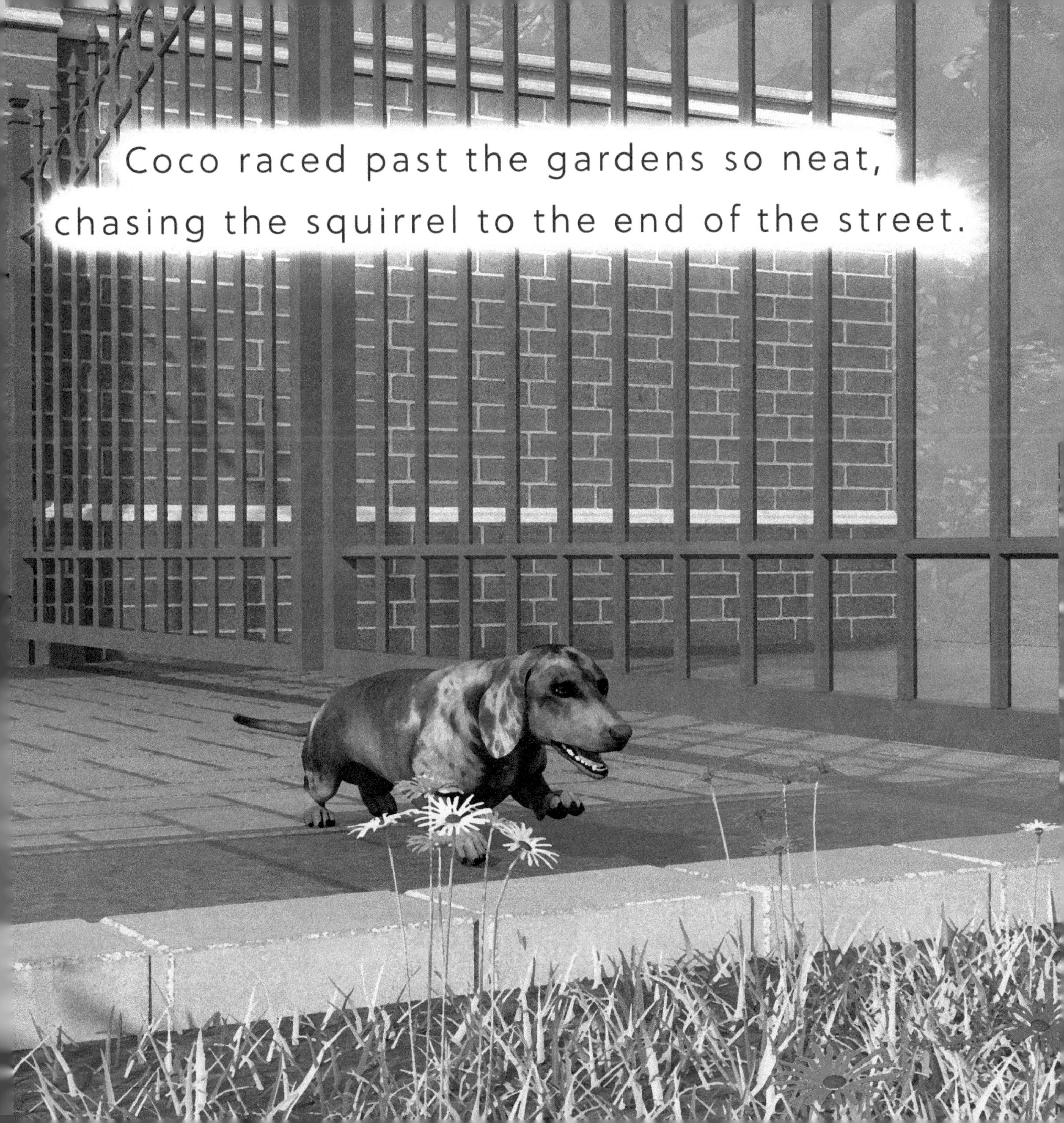
Coco raced past the gardens so neat,
chasing the squirrel to the end of the street.

Into the playground the two did run,
running through the legs of Sofie's mum.

Racing past the climbing frame,
Coco barked, "I love this game."

The squirrel ran into the deep, dark woods.
Coco whimpered, "This can't be good.

It's really scary and frightening in there,
but I'm big, brave, and never scared."

The trees in the
woods were tall and dark.
Coco tried her best to bark.

The squirrel was
gone and she was alone.
Coco had no idea how to get home.

Honey called out,
"Are you hiding in there?"
"Yes," cried Coco, "I'm right over here."

"I was lost and
afraid. I didn't know what to do.
I'm really very happy to finally see you."

Honey said, "It's okay to be scared.
I was also worried when
we were back there."

"You were scared too?" Coco asked. "But you're so big and brave," she gasped.

"Whenever I get stuck
and don't know where to go,
I find someone I can trust,
someone I know.
Even though we don't always agree,
you can always ask for help from me."

"I'm so glad you're
here and helped me get back.
I know I shouldn't have run
away like that."

Honey smiled, her eyes filled with glee.
"I'm just delighted you're back
home safe and with me."

Spot the difference

Can you find the 5 differences?

Honey and Coco
find the ducklings

Honey and Coco were
playing in the flowerbed,

looking for all the hues:
yellow, blue, and red.

A duck waddled closer,
hopping through the brambles.

"Oh no, this isn't good.
Oh, what a shambles!"

Coco asked, "Can we help? You look like you're in quite a tizzy?"

The duck waddled past. "Can't play now, sorry, far too busy."

"I can't find my ten ducklings.
I must go, I must hurry."

Honey barked, "We'll help find
them, don't you worry."

Coco said, "I've found one
hiding in the daisies.

Don't worry Mother Duck, we'll
find all your feathered babies."

Two little ducklings hiding in the garden.

"Eight more to go. Let's go find them."

Three little ducklings hiding
by the frames for climbing.
"Seven still to find. Let's keep counting."

Four little ducklings
hiding by the bushes.

"Six left to go. I saw
more following the horses."

Five little ducklings hiding by the stable.

"Five more to find,
I think they're at the castle."

Six little ducklings hiding behind the wall.

"Four left to find, can we find them all?"

Seven little ducklings hiding by the trees.

"Three left to find, can we hurry, please?"

Eight little ducklings hiding in the court.

"Two left to find," Coco did report.

Nine little ducklings hiding by the pond.

"One left to find," Honey did respond.

Ten little ducklings
hiding by the shack.

"Now we've found you all,
please follow us back."

Ten little ducklings marching in a line.

Ten little ducklings looking quite divine.

"Thank you so much, you found every last duckling."

"You are very welcome, Mother Duck,
we both love helping."

Spot the difference

Can you find the 5 differences?

Get more free activity sheets

at www.ItsHoneyAndCoco.com/Freebies

Honey and Coco
help a calf

Honey and Coco were sleeping in the garden when someone wandered in, hoping to find them.

Although they had spots, just like Coco, they cast a much larger and longer shadow.

"Oh dear," the calf said.
"Oh, how I do love to roam,
but now I haven't a clue
how to get home.

I have wandered far and wandered wide."
"And now you are lost?" Honey replied.

"Don't worry," Coco said,
"we'll help you find your way.
Could you please describe
the place where you stay?"

"Yes," Honey said, "please
tell us all that you know.
It will help us decide
where next we should go."

The calf smiled, standing proud.
"My home is quiet. It isn't loud."

Honey said, "I have an idea.
Come on, follow me, we'll try over here."

"Could this be the right place?" Honey asked, standing by a bookcase.

The calf replied, "Although
this is quiet, I do agree,
my home has space to play near a tree.

"This is outside and not too far away,"
Honey said, "and there's
plenty of different places to play."

The calf replied, "Oh no,
this is far too bright and bold.
My home is plain and rather old."

Coco barked, stood by the castle wall,
"Could this be the right place after all?"

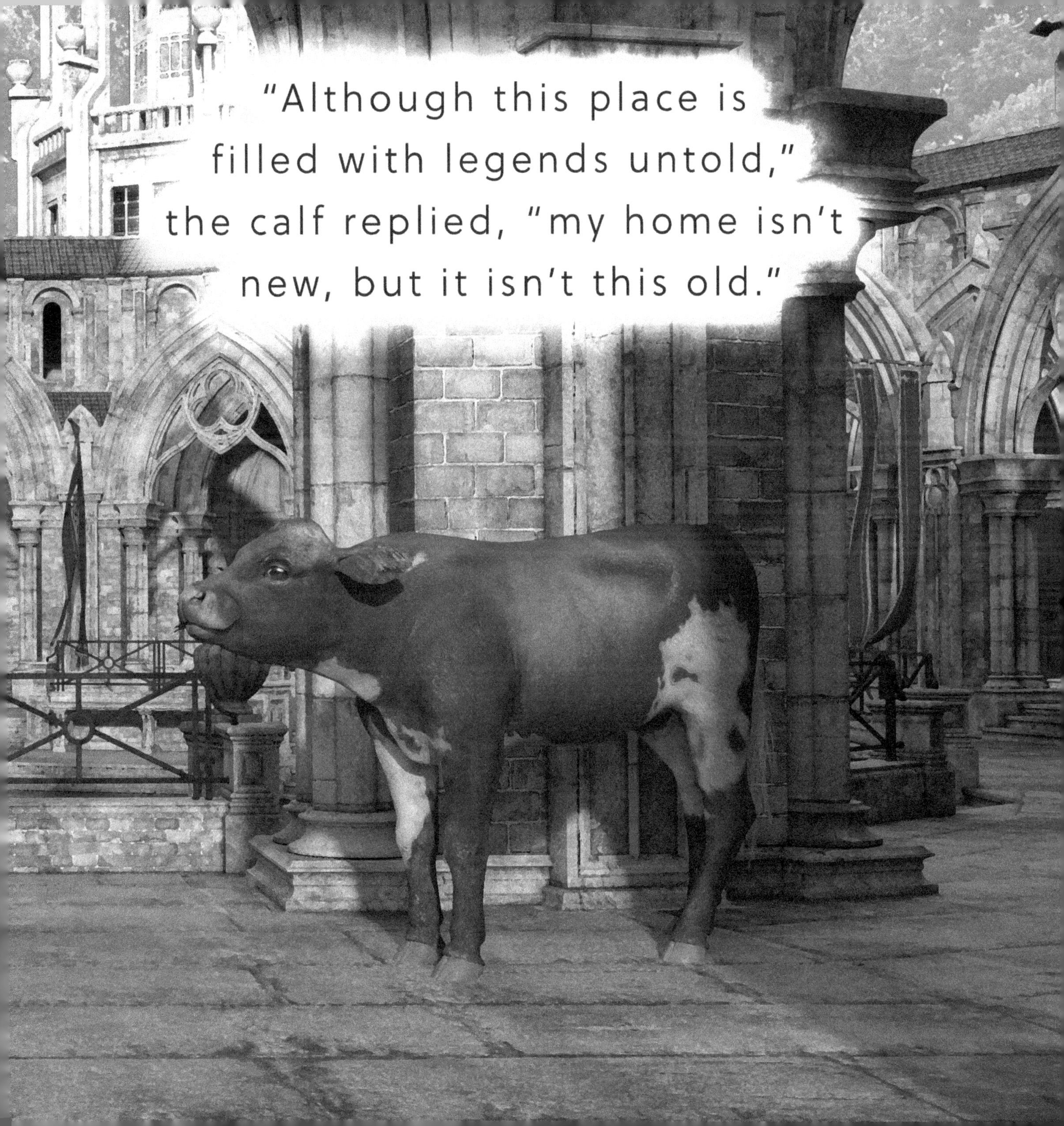
"Although this place is
filled with legends untold,"
the calf replied, "my home isn't
new, but it isn't this old."

The calf looked around.
"Could your home be the pond?"
Honey smiled and did respond.

"Oh no," the calf said, "this is far too wet.
I'm afraid water gets me rather upset."

"Here there is plenty of sunshine,"
Coco said, "more than
enough for any bovine."

"Oh no," the calf said, "this isn't right.
The desert gets far too cold at night."

Honey said, "There by
the fire is nice and warm.
A perfect place to hide from any storm."

"Oh no," the calf
said, "this is far too small.
My home has lots of grass
and only one small wall.

Coco said, "I hope it's not here.
This place fills me with fear."

"Oh no," the calf
said, "this is far too scary.
My home is definitely far more dairy."

Coco said, "Your home isn't loud, bold, wet, inside, small, or scary?"

"No," said the calf, "it's light, a little old, and definitely has a dairy."

Honey said,
"There's one place left to try.
It's behind the wall of the pigsty."

"Oh yes," the calf
said, "this is the farm.
You've brought me
back without any harm."

The calf smiled and said,
"Thank you for helping me to get home.
I will be more careful the next time I roam."

Honey said, watching
Coco jump off the haystack,
"We are just glad we got you back."

"You are more than
welcome, and we wish you goodbye."
Coco said, "If you roam past our
garden, please do come say hi."

The calf replied,
"On that you can depend.
I am so very lucky to
have you as my new friends."

Spot the difference
Can you find the 5 differences?

Get more free activity sheets
at www.ItsHoneyAndCoco.com/Freebies

Honey and Coco
Activity Sheets
Can you help Coco reach the rest of the missing presents in the middle of the maze?

Can you help Coco find the words below?

SQUIRREL **FOREST** **TREE**
NUT **WOOD** **HONEY**
COCO **RACE** **FRIENDSHIP**
HELPING

D	A	F	D	J	E	R	C	S	D	H	F	D	J	F
G	N	J	B	F	H	O	N	E	Y	S	J	S	D	F
X	F	U	D	D	J	B	G	V	F	O	R	E	S	T
M	V	B	T	K	F	X	N	C	N	J	M	O	L	R
Y	V	H	U	B	J	I	C	O	C	O	S	K	O	E
G	W	O	O	D	V	T	F	Q	G	F	C	W	R	E
M	L	E	N	P	Q	A	W	Z	S	D	X	D	E	T
N	J	I	H	E	L	P	I	N	G	U	H	B	Y	G
E	D	X	D	R	C	F	R	H	V	H	F	G	T	R
D	S	Z	E	C	W	A	Q	P	L	R	A	C	E	M
J	S	Q	U	I	R	R	E	L	I	Y	N	K	O	T
U	H	V	B	Y	C	G	U	V	T	F	C	R	D	X
W	D	F	R	I	E	N	D	S	H	I	P	S	D	E
Q	A	Z	W	S	C	E	B	D	R	F	V	Z	T	G
I	L	U	K	I	Y	M	J	S	U	T	Y	R	B	H

Can you help the calf reach their home in the middle of the maze?

Can you help Coco find the words below?

HONEY	**COCO**	**DAISIES**
FIND	**LOST**	**DUCKLING**
BUSHES	**STABLES**	**POND**
	HELPING	

P	T	Y	R	W	Q	L	K	J	H	G	F	D	M	N
M	H	L	D	A	I	S	I	E	S	Z	X	C	V	B
K	O	N	H	J	B	V	Y	G	V	T	F	R	D	X
J	N	K	M	L	P	W	S	T	A	B	L	E	S	S
B	E	H	V	Y	G	C	T	F	X	L	O	S	T	R
V	Y	H	B	J	N	K	M	L	P	Q	W	Z	S	D
H	Y	G	V	P	T	F	C	R	D	X	G	Z	W	Q
K	C	O	C	O	N	M	L	B	U	S	H	E	S	P
J	N	H	B	N	Y	G	V	T	F	C	R	D	X	F
B	H	N	J	D	M	K	M	L	P	Q	W	Z	S	I
H	Y	G	D	U	C	K	L	I	N	G	V	T	F	N
N	H	M	L	K	P	Q	W	Z	S	X	D	R	C	D
F	G	S	Y	H	J	D	H	K	D	C	B	Q	L	M
R	Y	H	E	L	P	I	N	G	G	H	N	J	K	P
F	D	B	G	W	R	Q	T	C	F	J	K	S	D	L

When you have finished ask a grown up to help you cut along this line

Use the box to add your name or a message for people to see when they approach your door

Complete the picture by connecting the dots

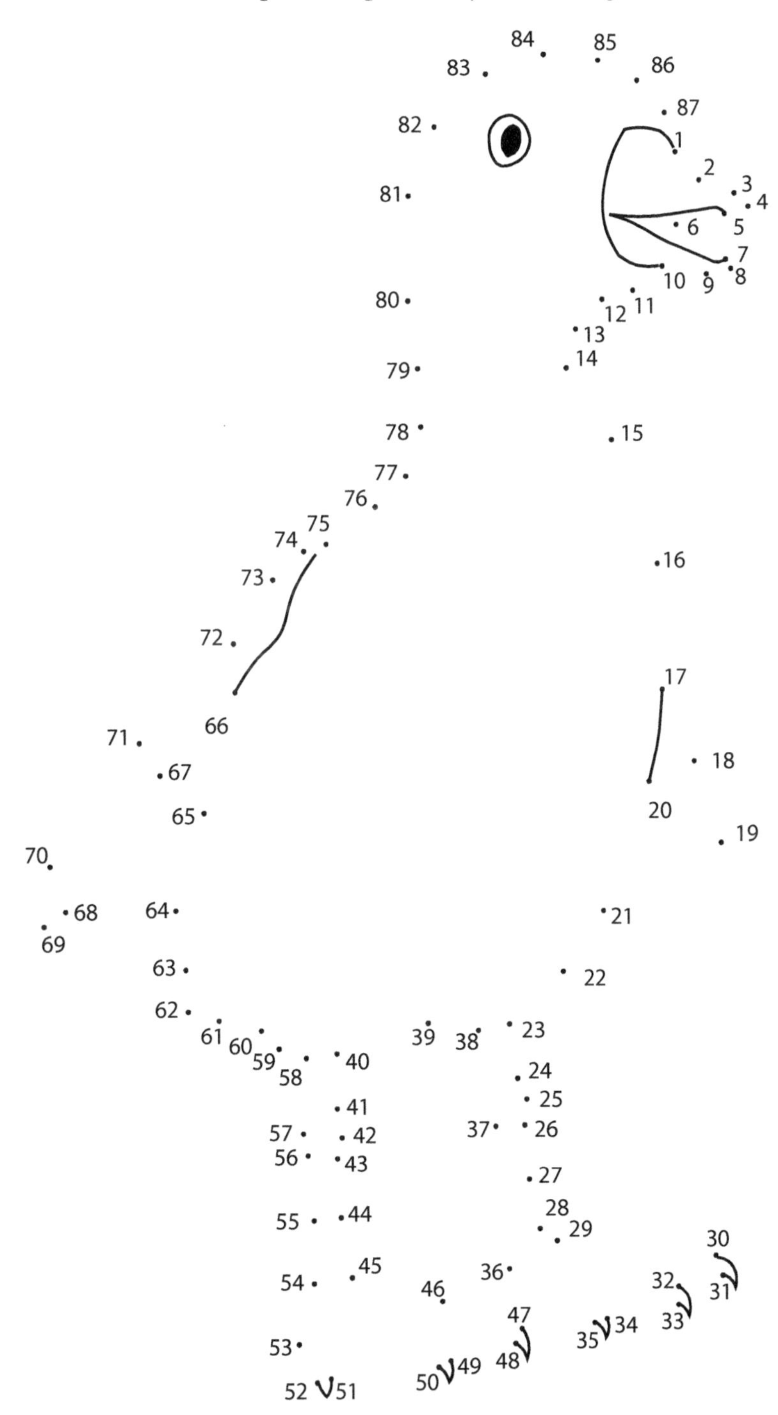

CPSIA information can be obtained
at www.ICGtesting.com
Printed in the USA
BVHW022031030221
599237BV00011B/1599